Hot Fudge

by **James Howe**

illustrated by **Jeff Mack**

Ready-to-Read

Aladdin

New York London Toronto Sydney

Harold is a special dog in many ways. He reads, he writes, and he loves chocolate. But chocolate is not a good food for most dogs; in fact, it makes them sick. Share your chocolate with people only. And give your dog another kind of treat—one that's just right for him or her.

ALADDIN PAPERBACKS
An imprint of Simon & Schuster Children's Publishing Division
1230 Avenue of the Americas, New York, NY 10020
Text copyright © 1990, 2004 by James Howe
Illustrations copyright © 2004 by Jeff Mack
Text adapted by Heather Henson from *Hot Fudge* by James Howe.
All rights reserved, including the right of reproduction in whole or
in part in any form.
ALADDIN PAPERBACKS, READY-TO-READ, and colophon are
registered trademarks of Simon & Schuster, Inc.
Also available in an Atheneum Books for Young Readers hardcover
edition.
Designed by Abelardo Martínez
The text of this book was set in Century Old Style.
The illustrations for this book were rendered in acrylic.
Manufactured in the United States of America
First Aladdin Paperbacks edition March 2006
10 9 8 7 6 5 4 3 2 1
The Library of Congress has cataloged the hardcover edition as
follows:
Howe, James, 1946-
Hot fudge / James Howe ; illustrated by Jeff Mack.
p. cm. — (Bunnicula and friends ; #2)
Summary: The Monroe family animals suspect that Bunnicula is up
to his old tricks when a pan of fudge turns white.
ISBN 0-689-85725-X (hc.)
[1. Fudge—Fiction. 2. Chocolate—Fiction. 3. Dogs—Fiction.
4. Cats—Fiction. 5. Rabbits—Fiction. 6. Vampires—Fiction.]
I. Mack, Jeff, ill. II. Title. III. Series.
PZ7.H8372Hml 2004
[Fic]—dc21 2003005570
 ISBN-13: 978-0-689-85750-8 (pbk.)
ISBN-10: 0-689-85750-0 (pbk.)

To Ellen Krieger—
for the many years of friendship
and the many pounds of chocolate
we have shared
—J. H.

To Mo, Kathleen, and Liz
—J. M.

CHAPTER 1:

Sweet Dreams

My name is Harold. I am a dog. I live with the Monroes. Toby and Pete and Mr. and Mrs. Monroe.

Toby is my favorite Monroe.

He lets me sleep in his bed, and he lets me share his snacks.

Friday nights are special.

Toby gets to stay up late.

He reads books and he eats snacks.

The books aren't bad, but the snacks are delicious.

"Chocolate is my favorite," Toby says.

Chocolate is my favorite, too. I get to have only a little bit, though.

That's because Mrs. Monroe read in a book once that chocolate might not be good for dogs.

So Toby lets me lick the sticky brown chocolate off his fingers. That way he won't get sticky brown smudges on the pages of his library books.

"Good job, Harold!" he says.

For some reason, they don't like sticky brown smudges down at the library.

When Toby gets tired, he brushes his teeth.

Then he turns out the light and says, "Good night, Harold. Sweet dreams."

And that's exactly what I have.

Sweet dreams filled with sweet chocolate.

But this Friday night was different.
Toby said good night like always.

Then he whispered in the dark,
"Wait until tomorrow, Harold. Yum,
yum. Just wait."

Now, I love to sleep almost as
much as I love to eat. That is the only
reason I was able to fall asleep that
night.

Yum, yum. Just wait. What did
Toby mean?

CHAPTER 2:

No Yum, Yum

All night long I dreamed about chocolate.

In the morning I woke up thinking about chocolate.

I could almost taste it.

I could almost smell it.

"Hey, I *can* smell it!" I said to myself. FUDGE!

Mr. Monroe was making his famous fudge!

Yum, yum.

That's what Toby meant the night before!

I jumped out of bed and rushed downstairs.

Mr. Monroe was in the kitchen
mixing up the fudge.

My friends Chester and Howie were there, too. They were busy eating their breakfast.

"Chester! Howie!" I yelled.

"What's the matter now?" Chester gulped.

"How can you eat that stuff when there's fudge in the air?"

"Because the fudge is in the air, not in our bowls, and we're hungry," Chester said.

Chester thinks he's so smart.

But he had a point.

"Move over," I said. I was hungry, too. Especially after all my chocolate dreams.

I wolfed down my food. Then I started begging. Howie joined me.

We whimpered.

We whined.

We rolled over.

We wagged our tails.

We tried to look cute.

Nothing worked.

"Have you no shame?" Chester asked.

"We're dogs," I explained. "Begging is one of the things dogs do best."

"Well, I'm glad I'm a cat," Chester said.

"As if rubbing up against people's legs when you want something is any better!" I replied.

Chester stuck up his nose and walked away.

I went back to begging.

"Nice try, guys," Mr. Monroe said at last. "But this fudge isn't for you."

Howie and I looked at each other. Not for us? What did he mean?

I tried one more time.

A whimper, a whine, and a wag.

But Mr. Monroe was one tough cookie.

He put the pan of fudge on the kitchen counter to cool. And all we got was a pat on the head.

Yum, yum, indeed!

CHAPTER 3:

Alone with the Fudge

After the Monroes finished their breakfast, things got crazy.

Everyone started running around and shouting and banging doors.

"I'm going to be late!" Pete yelled.

"I'm going to be late!" Toby screamed.

"We're all going to be late!" Mrs. Monroe sighed.

It was a typical Saturday morning.

Chester and Howie and I just tried to stay out of the way.

At last Mr. Monroe called, "Let's go!"
and everybody headed out the door.

"Good-bye, Harold!"

"Good-bye, Chester!"

"Good-bye, Howie!"

"Good-bye, Bunnicula!"

Bunnicula is the other pet in the
Monroe family. He's a bunny. Chester
says he's a vampire bunny.

Now that the Monroes were gone, the house got really quiet. Howie and I found ourselves alone in the kitchen.

Alone with a plate of fudge.

"Do you think we are being tested?" Howie asked.

"Yes," I said. "And we're about to flunk. Let's get out of here."

We ran to find Chester. He was in his
favorite chair, reading the newspaper.

There's something you should know
about Chester.

He likes to read. It gives him a lot of
funny ideas. Sometimes those funny
ideas get us into trouble.

"Listen to this!" Chester gasped. "There is a burglar on the loose. And he's been stealing things in this neighborhood!"

"So?" I asked.

"So we are going to have to guard the house!" Chester cried. "That's what pets are for."

"I thought pets are for loving and snuggling and rolling around with on the floor," I said.

"Yes, but we're also supposed to guard the house," Chester replied.

"I'd rather snuggle," Howie whimpered.

So would I. But I knew it was impossible to argue with Chester. Once his mind is made up, that's the end of it.

So Howie guarded the front door.

Chester went to the upstairs window.
I sat by the kitchen door. Near the
fudge.

CHAPTER 4:

Two Big Bangs

If you must know, guarding a house is pretty boring.

In no time I was sound asleep.

I was having the most wonderful dream when something woke me.

It was a big BANG!

"Chester!" I yelped.

Chester came running.

"I heard it, I heard it!" he said.

Howie poked his head in the door.
"Heard what?" he asked with a yawn.

I couldn't help it. I yawned, too.

"Don't tell me you two have been
sleeping!" Chester cried.

"Okay, we won't tell you," Howie said.

"They should call them dognaps,
not catnaps!" Chester sniffed.

Then his eyes got very big.

"Don't you know what has happened?" he gasped.

Howie and I looked at each other and shook our heads.

"The burglar has been here!" Chester screamed. "The fudge is missing!"

"Missing?" I gasped.

"Stolen!" said Chester.

"Stolen?" Howie asked. "You mean it's *hot fudge*?!"

"Yes!" Chester cried. "But the burglar can't be far away! Let's get him!"

We were just about to dash out the pet door when something caught my eye. It was the pan of fudge! But it was on the windowsill instead of on the counter.

"Wait," I said. "The fudge isn't gone. It just moved!"

"Who moved it?" Chester asked.

"I don't know, but let's see if it's all there," I suggested.

I put my front paws on the windowsill
and looked at the pan. I could hardly
believe my eyes!

"It's turned white!" I said.

"White?" Chester gasped. "Now we
know who's been messing with the
fudge!"

Chester dashed through the door
into the living room. Howie and I were
right behind him.

Bunnicula was sound asleep in
his cage.

"Don't be fooled," Chester whispered.
"He's just pretending to be asleep."

"Is he really a vampire?" Howie asked.

Howie wasn't around when the Monroes first brought Bunnicula home.

"Is he really a vampire?" Chester repeated. "Do dogs like bones?"

Howie and I looked at each other.

"Yes," we both answered.

"Well, Bunnicula really is a vampire bunny. He sucks the juice out of vegetables and turns them white!"

"I've never seen any white vegetables," Howie said.

"That's because the last time it happened was before you came to live with us, Howie. Now the Monroes give him vegetable juice. But that doesn't mean he wouldn't attack vegetables if he had the chance!" Chester said.

Howie looked confused. I knew how he felt. It was often confusing talking to Chester.

"But why would Bunnicula attack the fudge?" I asked.

"Maybe he has a sweet fang," Chester said.

"But what about that bang we heard?" I wanted to know.

Before anyone could answer, there was another loud BANG!

We rushed back to the kitchen.

This time the fudge was gone.
Really gone!

CHAPTER 5:

The Candy Burglar

We all rushed out the pet door.
"There he is!" Chester shouted.
The burglar was running down the street. He was dressed in a strange white coat and white hat.
We chased after him.

"What kind of thief would steal candy, anyway?" I wanted to know.

"A candy burglar!" Chester yelled.

As we ran, Howie yipped out warnings to the neighbors.

"Guard your gumdrops! Lock up your licorice!"

"We've almost got him!" Chester cried.

We were closing in on him!
We had him!
The candy burglar had fallen!
We had captured . . .

Toby!

"What's the matter with you guys?"
Toby cried.

"Are you nuts?"

Then he started laughing.

"Just nuts about chocolate, huh, Harold?"

Toby gave me a pat.

"Well, if it's chocolate you want, follow me!"

We followed him to the end of the block.

I could hardly believe my eyes.

There, right in front of the library, were tables covered with . . .

Cakes and cookies. Candy and cupcakes.

And chocolate. Everywhere.

"We were in such a rush this morning, we forgot the fudge!" Toby was saying. "Isn't this cool? I wish I could eat everything, don't you, Harold?"

I didn't know whether to whimper or pant. I did both.

"That still doesn't explain the two bangs!" Chester mumbled.

Toby seemed to understand. "I could only carry one pan at a time. So I had to make two trips," he said.

He put the pan of fudge on the table with all the other pans of fudge.

"That still doesn't explain why the fudge is white!" Chester grumbled.

"I guess you guys deserve a treat," Toby said. "Try some of this. Dad says it's a new recipe. White chocolate fudge."

White chocolate fudge?

I looked at Chester. "So you think Bunnicula has a sweet fang, do you?"

Chester shrugged and changed the subject.

"If you ask me, if it's not brown, it's not chocolate," he said.

If you ask *me*, cats are way too fussy.

Toby gave each of us a little taste.

"Yum," Howie said.

"Yum," I sighed.

"I'd rather have catnip," Chester sniffed.

That night there were leftovers.
It wasn't Friday, but it was special.
"Sweet dreams, Harold," Toby said.
And that's just what I had.
Sweet dreams.